Black Beauty

Retold by
Jo Franklin

Illustrated by
Joëlle Dreidemy

ARCTURUS

For Eleanor and Cedric—JF.

To Willow and Rowan, with love—JD.

ARCTURUS

This edition published in 2021 by Arcturus Publishing Limited
26/27 Bickels Yard, 151–153 Bermondsey Street,
London SE1 3HA

Writer: Jo Franklin
Illustrator: Joelle Dreidemy
Designer: Jeni Child
Editor: Sebastian Rydberg
Art Director: Jessica Crass

ISBN: 978-1-78828-683-1
CH006277NT
Supplier 24, Date 1220, Print run 11020

Printed in Malaysia

Contents

CHAPTER 1

My Early Life

When I was a foal, I lived with my mother in a beautiful meadow with a pond of clear water in the corner. During the day, I ran by my mother's side, and at night,

I lay close by her. When it was hot, we stood under the trees in the shade, and when it was cold, we had a snug stable to keep us warm and dry.

My mother's name was Duchess. Our master had many animals, but he loved her best of all. Every day that he came to see us, he petted her as if she were his own child. She was gentle and wise, and he loved her for it. So did I.

In the field next to us lived six young colts. They were older than me, but I had great fun galloping around the field with them. Sometimes, the game got a little rough, and the colts kicked out as they played and tried to nip each other's necks. One day, when our game became too lively, my mother whinnied for me to come to her.

"You must listen to me carefully, my young son. The colts are good colts, but they are carthorse colts, and they have no manners. You have been well born. Your father was a cup winner at the races, and you have never seen me kick or bite." She nudged my neck with her soft muzzle to make sure I was listening properly. "I hope you will grow up gentle and good like your parents. You must work hard with a good will, whoever your master is. Pick your feet up well when you trot, and never bite or kick when you are playing."

"Yes, Mother," I bowed my head with shame. "I won't play rough with the colts again."

My mother nudged my ear, which was her way of saying she trusted me to keep my word. I promised myself that I would always try to be a good horse like her.

When I was four years old, I was ready to be broken in. This was the training I needed to become an adult horse. I'd always worn a soft head collar and was used to being led, but now I had to learn to wear a leather bridle and a saddle, so that anyone could ride me.

At first, I didn't like the cold steel bit that was pushed into my mouth, but my master spoke softly to me, which made me less scared. I didn't like the feel of the hard saddle, either, but after a few weeks, I was proud to wear a saddle and carry my master.

Before I could go out onto the road, I had to have shoes to protect my feet from the hard stones. Master took me to the blacksmith, who made iron shoes that fitted my feet perfectly. My feet felt stiff and heavy at first, but before long, I was used to them and picked my feet up smartly as my mother had told me to do.

One day, my master took me to a nearby farmer. I was turned out into a field on my own. I didn't know why I had been sent there, but the grass was tasty, so I was happy

enough. Suddenly, a thundering monster hurtled out of nowhere and roared alongside the hedge. Smoke belched from the funnel on the back of its head. Instead of legs, the monster had wheels that sped around faster than any cart.

I'd never
seen anything
like it, and I
ran to the far
corner of the
field in case
the monster leaped over the hedge and
gobbled me up. But the iron monster
sped into the distance without even
looking at me.

Many monsters passed the field.
Some were slow and lumbering. Others
screeched their
whistles as they
passed by. None
of the monsters
even glanced in
my direction,
and I realized that

a train on a track was absolutely nothing to fear.

*

The best part of my training was when my master drove me in a double harness with my mother. She showed me how to behave and gave me instructions as we worked together.

"A horse never knows who may buy them," she said, as we trotted along. "But you must always be the best you can be whoever your master or mistress should be."

Once my training was complete, I was taken to my new home at Squire Gordon's stables. The stables were airy and clean, and I felt very privileged to be led into a large box stall where I didn't need to be tied up.

The sides were topped with iron rails that were low enough for me to see through.

In the next stall stood a fat, dappled pony with a thick mane and tail.

"How do you do?" I asked politely through the rails. "What is your name?"

The pony turned to look at me through the bars, holding his head up high. "My name is Merrylegs, and I carry the young ladies on my back because

I am so handsome. Are you going to live next to me?"

"Yes, I think so." I felt a little shy because I was new, and he was so confident.

"Well, I hope you are better tempered than the other one." Merrylegs tossed his head toward the stall on the other side to me. "That one bites."

Just then, another horse looked over from the stall behind me. She was a tall, chestnut-brown mare, with a white blaze down the middle of her face.

"So, you are the one who has taken my box."

"I beg your pardon," I said politely but stepping back, so that the chestnut horse couldn't bite me. "I have not taken anything. The man put me in here, and I wish to live in peace with you all."

The grumpy horse snorted and moved over to the other side of her box.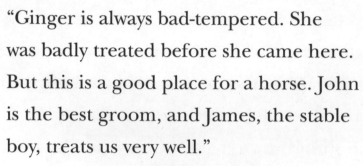

"Don't mind her," Merrylegs said. "Ginger is always bad-tempered. She was badly treated before she came here. But this is a good place for a horse. John is the best groom, and James, the stable boy, treats us very well."

Before I could answer, my stable door was opened, and John, the groom, led me out into the yard where the squire and Mrs. Gordon were waiting.

"Well, what do you think?" the squire asked his wife.

"He's wonderful!" Mrs. Gordon said, as she ran her hand along my back.

I could feel how kind she was by her gentle touch. Merrylegs was right. This was a good home.

"I know the perfect name for him." She leaned in close and pushed her face to my ear just like my mother had done. "Black Beauty," she spoke softly. "I hope you like that name."

I whinnied softly in reply, hoping that she knew I liked the name and new home.

CHAPTER 2
A Very Happy Family

Everyone was right. Squire Gordon's stables were the best home a horse could hope for. For the first time, I had two friends in Merrylegs and Ginger (who turned out to be not so grumpy after all). John and James took excellent care of us. The Squire and Mrs. Gordon were the perfect master and mistress. We were one big happy family.

One day, John hitched me to the dog cart because the Squire needed to go out on business. It had rained all night, and the sky was still dark with clouds. The river raced high and furious, almost touching the planks of the bridge as it flowed away.

"Good day to you, Squire." The man at the tollgate stepped out, pulling his muffler over his chin against the brisk wind. "Don't worry if the water splashes up between the planks. It is normal for this bridge."

I trotted across the bridge on John's command, even though I could see the river rushing beneath us. It was only water, and we had a sturdy bridge to keep us safe.

It was late in the afternoon when we made our way homeward again. It was nearly nightfall when we got to the bridge. The river had risen further, and the water lapped over the middle exactly as the toll man had said it would.

"Come on, Beauty, let's get home," John commanded, as he steered the dog cart toward the bridge.

I had never refused John or disobeyed my master's orders, but the moment my hooves touched the bridge, I knew

something was wrong. I pulled up sharply and wouldn't take another step.

"It's only a touch of water," James said and shook the reins as the sign for me to go on, but I flatly refused to move.

"Stop!" A voice called out from the other side of the bridge. "The bridge has broken." The toll man swayed his lantern back and forward. "Turn back!"

The light from his lantern lit up the bridge. The side rail upriver was still in place, but I couldn't see the other rail at all. The river was angry and powerful as it crashed into the broken planks we had driven over this morning. The middle of the bridge had been swept clean away.

John jumped down and took my harness to lead me around to the road that ran beside the riverbank.

"Thank you, Beauty," Squire Gordon said, as we pulled into the stable at home. "You saved our lives today. We would have been swept away if we had tried to cross the bridge. John, make sure you take special care of this horse tonight."

"I will do, sir." John patted my neck and gave me some crushed beans with my oats. We were safely home, and I'd never been so pleased to see my stable. I was lucky to be alive.

If my master had business farther away from home, Ginger and I would take him together in the bigger carriage. Sometimes, we would spend the night at a different stable. John or James went with us and worked with the local stable hands to make sure we were well cared for.

One night, when James was settling us into a strange stable, he asked the local stable hand to help him.

"Run up the ladder, and drop some hay into the horse's rack, will you?" James asked the young man. "But leave your pipe down here, please."

It was a common thing for men to smoke pipes, but Squire Gordon had a strict ban on smoking in the stables.

I heard the boy step on the beams above my head, and he put the hay into my rack as he was asked.

James looked in at us last thing at night, and then the stable yard fell silent for the night.

I slept for a while but woke up feeling uncomfortable. The air was thick, and I could hardly breathe. There was a strange rushing, crackling sound in the barn above us. I'd never heard that noise before, and it made me tremble with terror.

The other horses were awake, too, and some pulled at their halters while others stamped nervously. We didn't know what was happening, but we were all afraid.

At last, I heard some steps outside, and the door flew open. A strange groomsman came in and untied us all. I could smell the fear on him, and even though we should have all followed him obediently, we were too afraid. We were surrounded by an unknown danger, and we didn't trust this man.

The rushing sound overhead grew louder, and a red light flickered on the wall.

"Fire!" A cry went up outside, and at that moment, the flames turned into a raging furnace above us. Next thing I knew, James was right beside me.

"Come along, Beauty." He spoke cheerily in my ear as if nothing was wrong. "Time to be out of here." He slipped my bridle on and wrapped a scarf over my eyes. I couldn't see anything, but I trusted James, so I let him guide me into the fresh air.

Once out in the yard, he threw my reins to someone else and dashed back into the fire.

Ginger was still in the stable with the flames. Smoke poured out thicker than ever, and I heard a crash of something falling inside. I let out a shrill whinny calling to James and Ginger.

Next moment, they were at the door. James's face was dirty with soot, and Ginger choked violently, her eyes white with terror.

James led us safely to the other side of the market square just as the fire engine arrived.

"Thank you," Ginger coughed when her voice returned.

"Me?" I said.

"Yes, Black Beauty. I wouldn't have come out of that stable if I hadn't heard your call. You saved my life."

"Why, that's what friends are for," I said.

CHAPTER 3

A Midnight Emergency

The Squire and Mrs. Gordon were very impressed with James's bravery that night.

"Most horses would freeze in terror," the Squire said to James the next morning. "You have a real skill with horses, and I am going to recommend you to Lord Wilson, who is looking for a new head groom."

"Thank you, sir, I'm very grateful to you," James blushed as if he was embarrassed, but he didn't need to be. He had saved both me and Ginger that night.

We were all pleased for him when he was offered the job, but we were also sad because we would never see him again.

"Who will take my job here?" James asked John.

"Joe Green, who lives at the lodge."

"That kid?" James said. "He knows nothing about horses."

"He knows nothing now, but he'll learn. Beauty and I will teach him." John patted me gently as he walked past. It was good that John would always look after me, even if James was working far away.

The next day, little Joe Green started work. He was too short to groom me and Ginger, so he began brushing Merrylegs.

"He keeps mauling me about," Merrylegs complained after the first time Joe tried to groom him, but after another week, Merrylegs admitted that Joe was already getting better at caring for him.

Eventually, James had to say goodbye. He patted each of us and thanked us for being such great horses to work with. Of course, we couldn't tell him how grateful we were to be cared for by him, but I think he knew. As he walked away, he dragged his feet and dipped his head low with his carpetbag thrown across his shoulders.

John now had to train Joe Green to be a good stable hand.

*

A few days later, I was settling down for the night, when a cry went up, and I heard feet running outside. John rushed into my stable.

"Quick, Beauty, Mrs. Gordon has taken ill, and we must fetch the doctor before it is too late."

John saddled me, and we started off in the darkness.

He didn't need to use his whip or spurs. I sensed the urgency. Mrs. Gordon was my lovely mistress who had given me the name "Black Beauty" and now she was in danger. I wanted to help her.

The air was frosty, and the moon bright, which meant there was nothing stopping me from galloping at full speed. John pulled me up when we reached the bridge, and I'm sure he would have taken the second half of the journey at a steadier pace, but I didn't want to slow down. My mistress needed the doctor right away, so I galloped on until we arrived in the town.

John thumped on the doctor's front
door. The doctor poked his head
out the window in his
nightcap and gown.

"Mrs. Gordon
is very ill, sir," John
called up. "Please
come quickly."

"Just a moment,
I'll be right down."
The doctor shut the window and soon
came downstairs, tucking his nightgown
into his breeches. "But I don't have a
horse. Mine has been out all day. Can I
take yours?"

"I was supposed to rest him and ride
him home in the morning," John said.
"He has galloped the whole way here."
I sensed the edginess in John's voice.

I felt my heart pounding and my skin burning hot, but still, I willed John to agree. My mistress needed the doctor, and I was the horse to take him to her.

"Okay," John said. "But take care. He's a fine, loyal horse, and we care about him a great deal."

The doctor nodded, and we rode back home. The journey took longer than on the outward run because the doctor was heavier and not such a good horseman as John, but we arrived at last and the doctor rushed inside to my mistress.

I was glad to be home. My legs shook, and I could barely stand. Since John was still in the town, the only person to care for me was little Joe Green. No one had taught him how to care for an overheated horse, but he did the best he could.

"You're too hot," he said as he rubbed
me down. "I'm not going to give you a
blanket, so that you can cool down." He
gave me a bucket of ice cold water, which
I gulped down immediately. Then, he
left me alone thinking that he had done
everything right.

Soon, I began to shake, and my body felt deadly cold. My legs and chest ached, and I felt sore all over. I needed that warm blanket, and I needed John, but I was all alone. I lay down in my straw and tried to sleep.

Later, I remember John being with me. I couldn't tell him how bad I was feeling, but he knew anyway. He covered me with three snug cloths and fed me some warm gruel. Eventually, I fell asleep.

I was now very ill.

John nursed me night and day. He slept in my stable, so that he could check on me during the night. He didn't speak to Joe Green the whole time.

"My poor Beauty," my master cried when he came to see me. "You saved your mistress's life, but look what it has done to you."

I don't know how long I was sick. Merrylegs and Ginger were moved to a different part of the stable because any sound startled me.

It was a lonely time.

Young Joe Green was terribly upset. He'd done his best but didn't know how to care for horses back then.

I lay ill in the stable, and my mistress lay ill in the house.

After a few weeks, my fever passed, and I started getting better. Eventually, I was fit enough to go out for a steady ride. Joe Green rode me as he was the lightest groom, and he treated me respectfully.

My mistress didn't make such a good recovery. The doctor said she needed to be moved to a warmer country.

The house was to be shut up while she and the master were away. That meant that Merrylegs, Ginger, and I needed new homes, and John and Joe had to leave us to find new jobs.

The day Mrs. Gordon left the house, she had to be carried to the carriage because she was too weak to walk. Ginger and I drove her to the train station.

Everyone cried as she said goodbye, and it was a sad party that returned to the house for the last time.

The next day, Merrylegs went to live at the vicarage, and Ginger and I left for our new home at Earlshall, uncertain what lay ahead of us.

CHAPTER 4

Problems at Earlshall

I wasn't looking forward to changing
homes, but Ginger was coming with me.
We were given bright stables next to
each other, and the other horses were
pleasant enough, but things started to
go wrong as soon as we were hitched
to the carriage for the first time. At
Earlshall, they used the check rein,
which was a horrible thing that I'd heard
about but never experienced myself.

The check rein was an extra strap
that fitted from the bit in my mouth,
over my head, and attached to the
harness across my back. It stopped me
from lowering my head. It was the fashion
to have horses' heads held high, but it

was terribly painful, especially if we had to pull the carriage uphill.

Squire Gordon had never used the check rein, but Ginger knew exactly what it was and how badly it hurt.

check rein

To begin with, Ginger didn't complain. York, the coachman, knew we weren't used to this rein, so he didn't tighten it too much, but her ladyship wasn't happy.

"For goodness' sake, York, tighten that rein. I will not have the horses with their heads so low," she complained bitterly. I could feel Ginger's temper brewing as she stood beside me.

She fidgeted and shook her head,
knowing what was coming next. The
moment York released her rein to
shorten it, Ginger reared up. She was still
harnessed to the carriage, but that didn't
stop her bucking and kicking like a mad
thing. Somehow, she managed to jump
over the carriage pole. She ended up
lying on the floor with York lying on
her head to stop her rearing again.

In a mad frenzy, the grooms unbuckled
me to release me from the carriage, and

they led me back to the stable. I was
still trussed up in the check rein, and I
wanted to kick out just like Ginger, but I
knew that good horses didn't behave like
that. Eventually, Ginger was led back into
her box. She looked rather shocked. York
came over to me, his face red with anger.

"I hate these check reins," he said, as
he released me at last. "But I have to do
what her ladyship tells me."

Ginger was never put in the carriage again. She was used as a hunter instead, which is a different sort of hardship. Meanwhile, I had to wear the check rein every time I took out the carriage. I always returned to my stable with a sore tongue and aching back, and Ginger came back every night exhausted because she had been ridden hard across the fields.

When York went to London with his lordship, Reuben Smith was in charge. He was a first-rate driver and knew how to care for us if we were ill because he used to work for a veterinarian. He should have been head coachman, but unfortunately, he had a weakness for alcohol. Mostly, he avoided it, but sometimes he got tempted. He would drink too much and behave very badly.

One day, Reuben took me for a ride. We stopped at the White Lion, and I was cared for by the inn's own stable hand while Reuben went inside. When he came out, he was in a foul temper and could hardly walk straight.

"Excuse me, but I think your horse has a loose shoe," the stable hand said.

"It'll be all right. Out of my way." Reuben pushed the man aside and mounted me roughly. He rode me just as carelessly, digging his heels in and giving me a sharp swipe with the whip, even though I was going as fast as I could.

The roads were stony. My shoe loosened as we rode, until suddenly, it flew off. Any sensible horseman would have noticed, but Reuben Smith was too drunk to notice. We continued at a wild pace, and my shoeless foot became more and more painful as the sharp stones dug into it.

In the end, the pain was too great.
I stumbled suddenly and fell to my knees.
Reuben was flung off my back and landed
heavily by the side of the road.

I pulled myself to my feet, but my
knees were bleeding, and my foot was
so sore I couldn't put it down.
Reuben Smith didn't move.

After a while, I heard another horse approaching. It was Ginger pulling the dog cart. I neighed loudly, and soon she was by my side. Two men jumped down to help Reuben Smith, but sadly, it was too late for him.

"This horse has thrown him," one of the men said rudely.

His words cut as painfully as the whip. I had never thrown a rider in my life. Robert, a groom, came over, and the moment he saw my wounds, he knew that something was wrong.

"It's not Black Beauty's fault. There is a stone wedged in his foot. No wonder he went down, and look at the state of his knees."

They put poor Reuben in the cart, and I limped home with Robert.

Next morning, the farrier patched me up as best he could.

"His joints are okay," he said. "But he'll be scarred for life."

He was right. The wounds did heal, but now that I had ugly, scarred knees, my lord and lady didn't want me any longer.

And that is how I ended up in my first-ever horse fair.

CHAPTER 5

A Change of Fortune

There is a lot to see at a horse fair, and I'm sorry to say that not all of it is pleasant.

There were droves of shaggy Welsh ponies and many heavy horses in every shade and condition. There were fine horses showing off their paces in high

style with their grooms running by their side and young colts newly broken in.

In the background were a number of poor nags, sadly broken down from hard work. Their knees collapsed under them, and their back legs swung at every step. There were a number of horses like me, highbred but now fallen to a lower class because of an accident or blemish.

The horse dealers bragged and bargained all day. I was put together with some other useful-looking horses, and we had plenty of people examining us. First, they pulled my mouth open and looked into my eyes. Then, they felt my legs all the way down. Lastly, they'd ask me to walk around so they could see how I moved.

Many of these potential owners handled me carelessly, but one chap was different.

He wasn't a gentleman, but he spoke gently, and his quick eyes had a cheery look. After a hard bargain, he bought me, and I was very pleased to leave the fair with my new owner.

We rode a fair way through pleasant lanes and country roads and then came into London. The gas lamps were already lit. Streets went off to the right and to the left, all crossing each other for mile upon mile. I thought we'd never come to the end of it, and I kept thinking what a long way I'd come since I was a young foal running with my mother in the fields.

At last, we pulled up at one of the houses, and a woman and two children ran out to greet us.

"Is he gentle, Father?" the girl asked.

"As gentle as a kitten. Give him a pat."

My owner's wife gave me a lovely bran mash, and for the first time in a long time, I felt happy to call a place my home.

My new master's name was Gerry, and he was a London cab driver, or cabbie. His morning horse was called Captain, and I drove the cab in the afternoon. We all had Sunday off.

I certainly needed one rest day a week because my life as a cab horse was hard work. There were too many people, too many carriages and carts on the road, and too much noise. Luckily, I was in safe hands and soon learned to trust Gerry because he knew where we were going.

All afternoon, we went from one place to another, picking up passengers and taking them where they wanted to go. It was never-ending, but Gerry treated me and Captain well. We had plenty to eat, and I could have a cooling drink whenever I needed it.

His family were delightful. They petted me and groomed me every day, and I felt well loved again. So, the weeks sped by. There were six days of hard work; followed by one day's rest.

Christmas was a very busy time for cabbies. In the daytime, everyone was busy going from shop to shop buying presents; then they needed a cab to get home with their parcels. In the evenings, there were late parties.

Although it was an opportunity for Gerry to earn plenty, Christmas also coincided with the worst of the winter weather, which was not good for his health.

One night, we took some young gentlemen to a party and were instructed to wait outside, so that we could drive them home after the party. It was a cold night, and I could see my breath in the frosty air every time I breathed out. Gerry walked up and down swinging his arms to try and keep warm, but soon he was coughing. He wrapped himself in rugs and sat  on his box because cab drivers were not allowed to sit inside. His cough was so bad, the cab rattled with the force of it.

Eventually, the gentleman reappeared, and we drove them home. They paid Gerry a good fare, but it wasn't enough. My poor

master could
hardly talk. His
wife took him
inside, and his
son, Harry, gave
me a bran mash.

Gerry's chest was so bad, he couldn't
get out of bed, and he certainly couldn't
go back to work. Luckily, Harry knew
how to care for me, and I was grateful
for the rest because maybe if I had gone
out cabbing in that weather, I would have
become sick like Gerry.

My master did get better, but he
decided to give up cab driving. He found
a job in the countryside, but there was no
position for me. I was to be sold again, and
I couldn't help wondering who would want
an old horse with scarred knees like me.

CHAPTER 6

Another Life

At the sale, I was put in with all the old horses. The buyers and sellers didn't look much better off than the horses. Some of the buyers were hard-bitten, but there were others I would have been willing to serve, even if they were poor and shabby.

A gentleman farmer with a young boy

wandered over to look at us. I saw his eye rest on me, and I gave my tail a swish so he could see what a fine beast I used to be.

"He must have been a smart fellow in his day, Willie," the old man said to the boy. "Look at his nostrils and ears. And the shape of his neck. You're a well-bred old fellow." The old man patted my neck, and I put my nose out to him in answer to his kindness. The boy stroked my face.

"Could you buy him, Grandpapa? And make him well again?"

"I don't know, Willie. He might be past fixing."

But the young lad didn't give up. His grandfather asked for me to be walked around, and I did my very best to pick up my feet smartly and toss my head to show I still had a little spirit.

"I'll give you five pounds for him," the farmer said to the dealer.

I was so happy to be led away from the horse market. I made a silent wish for the other poor creatures I left behind and followed my new master home.

The master released me into a large meadow with a dry stable. Young Willie came and visited me every day with a generous helping of oats and hay. I soon grew stronger.

In the spring, my new master took me out in the light carriage, and I showed him exactly the horse I used to be. I trotted on, tossing my mane and tail as if I was still a colt.

"He's growing young again," the old man said, "thanks to you, Willie."

One day, the groom came to tend to me. He cleaned and dressed me with care. I guessed I was to be sold again. I didn't want to leave my lovely field, but I hoped that my master would ensure that I went to a good home.

I was taken to a village a couple of miles away, and we stopped outside a pretty house with nodding daffodils by the door.

Three ladies came out to look at me.
One was wrapped in a white shawl that
matched her hair. Her name was Miss
Bloomfield. The other ladies, Miss Laura
and Miss Emily, were younger but clearly
gentle and kind.

"Are you sure he's safe?" Miss
Bloomfield said. "His knees are scarred.
If he's been down once, he might go down

again and drag my carriage with him."

"I don't know what happened to him. It may have been an accident. He's never given me any trouble," my master told the ladies.

"I think we should ask Joseph," Miss Laura said.

A servant fetched their groom. He ran his hands over my back and legs like a true horseman. For a moment, I thought I was back at Squire Gordon's again with John and James because this groom treated me just as kindly.

The groom came around and examined my head. I looked in his eyes and could see a question there.

"You look like a horse I knew once— Black Beauty," he said. "He was a fine creature. I wonder where he is now."

"Black Beauty is a fine name," Miss Bloomfield said.

"He had a star on his forehead and one white foot just like this old fellow. He was the same height, too." The groom stood back and scratched his head. "I wonder if this could be the same horse."

He stepped forward and parted the hair on my back as if he was looking for something.

"Why, it is him! Look, that little spot of white hair. John used to call it Beauty's secret penny. This must be the horse I knew when I was a boy. Black Beauty, do you remember me? I am Joe Green. Have you forgiven me for nearly killing you all those years ago?"

I wouldn't have recognized his face because this Joe Green was a man with whiskers, but I recognized his smile.

"Do you know this horse?" Miss
Bloomfield asked.

"Yes, miss, and a finer, more loyal horse
you could never hope for. He fetched
the doctor when the mistress nearly died.
Galloped all night and saved her life."
He smiled, but I saw a hint of sadness in
his eyes as he
thought of
our mistress.
"Black
Beauty, I am
so glad to see
you again."

"I like a horse with a good history and
a good name. It would be my pleasure to
buy this horse from you. Welcome, Black
Beauty," Miss Bloomfield said.

The other two ladies broke into a round of applause. Joe patted my neck, and Willie hugged his Grandpapa.

And me? I whinnied and tossed my head a little at the joy of finding a place I could call home. I served Miss Bloomfield and the younger ladies loyally until the end of my days, and in return, Joe Green looked after me as carefully as John and James had done all those years ago.

ADVENTURE PARK

PIRATE PERIL

By Cavan Scott • Illustrated by Abby Ryder

Titles in the Adventure Park set

Dinosaur Danger

Monster Mayhem

Pirate Peril

Candy Crisis

Cosmic Chaos

Rainforest Riot

Medieval Madness

Pyramid Panic

Badger Publishing Limited,
Oldmedow Road, Hardwick Industrial Estate,
King's Lynn PE30 4JJ

Telephone: 01438 791037
www.badgerlearning.co.uk

2 4 6 8 10 9 7 5 3 1

Pirate Peril ISBN 978-1-78464-337-9

Text © Cavan Scott 2016
Complete work © Badger Publishing Limited 2016

Publisher: Susan Ross
Senior Editor: Danny Pearson
Editorial Coordinator: Claire Morgan
Illustration: Abby Ryder
Designer: Bigtop Design

Contents

Meet Emily. Her grandfather owns
Adventure Park. It's the best theme
park in the world!

Meet Jacob. He's Emily's best friend.

Meet Frank. He's Emily's pet hamster.

Together, they test Adventure Park's new rides.

Some of the rides are magical. Some of the
rides are scary. Some of the rides are dangerous.
But ALL of the rides are exciting!

Join Emily, Jacob and Frank on the
adventure of a lifetime.

Cast of Characters

Emily

Jacob

Frank

Vocabulary

saltcellar – a container for holding and sprinkling salt.

ocean – a large amount of sea.

pendulum – something that swings back and forth.

jabbed – poked at.

cutlass – a short sword that was used by sailors.

ridiculous – really silly.

tentacles – long, bendy legs used to grab things.

"Hang on!" yelled Emily.

"I am!" Jacob shouted.

The ship was tossing this way and that. The deck was slippery and the sails were tattered.

"We're going to be shipwrecked," Frank the hamster cried out.

"No, we're not," Emily said. "We just need to think of a way to escape!"

Beneath them, the sea monster roared!

But wait a minute! We've jumped straight to the middle of the story.

How did Emily, Jacob and Frank end up on a ship in the middle of the ocean? And why are they being attacked by a sea monster?

Well, it all started when Emily's grandfather appeared, wearing a pair of rollerblades.

Albert Sparkle-Trousers was the owner of Adventure Park.

He was very old.

He was very clever.

He had never tried using rollerblades before.

"Clear the deck!" he yelled as he raced towards Emily, Jacob and Frank.

Albert rammed straight into the children,
knocking them to the ground.

"Sorry!" said the old man. "Tricky things these
rollerblades!"

Jacob picked himself up. He had been eating a
bag of chips. Now the chips were scattered all
over the floor.

"They're ruined," Jacob groaned.

Frank ran over to a chip and popped it into his mouth.

"No they're not," the hamster said. "They just need a little salt!"

Frank pulled a saltcellar out of his cheek pouches and sprinkled salt over the scattered chips. He carried all kinds of things in his cheeks.

"Why are you in such a hurry, Grandad?" asked Emily.

"Because I'm about to open this," he said proudly. He pointed to a new ride nearby in the Park.

It was a huge pirate ship.

"What does it do?" Jacob said, looking at the ride.

"Oh it's simple," said Frank, who was a bit of a know-it-all. "The pirate ship swings on those giant arms, see?"

"Like a clock's pendulum, you mean?" Emily asked.

Frank nodded. "You won't catch me going on that!" he said. "Far too scary for this little hamster!"

"Time to get on," said Albert, shoving them onto the ride.

"You can be the first to try it out!"

"But, but, but…" complained Frank, but it was too late. Emily and Jacob strapped themselves in.

Frank hid inside Jacob's jacket.

The ride started, the pirate ship swinging one way and then the other.

It went faster and faster. Higher and higher.

"This is brilliant!" shouted Jacob.

Emily wasn't listening. She'd spotted a little man at the back of the ride.

He was wearing a long cloak and a large hat.

Suddenly, the stranger jumped up.

He threw off his cloak and Emily saw that he was standing on a small cannon!

He had a long, bushy beard, a patch over one eye and a hook for a hand.

Emily gasped. The man was a real pirate!

BOOM!

A cannonball shot out of the cannon.

It smashed through the rods that held the ship in place.

The pirate ship rocketed away from Adventure Park and out towards the sea.

With a huge SPLASH! it landed on the water.

"What did you do that for?" Frank squeaked from inside Jacob's jacket.

The pirate stomped over to them.

Emily noticed that he didn't just have one peg leg. This pirate had two!

"I'm Captain Wildbeard and this is my new ship!" he snarled.

His long, tangled beard dragged along the floor behind him.

"But what about us?" Emily asked.

Wildbeard jabbed his cutlass at them. "You're my new crew," he said.

"But we don't want to be your crew," Jacob said. "We want to go back to Adventure Park."

Wildbeard smiled a horrible smile. His teeth were rotten and black. "Then I hope you can swim, matey," he said. "You're a long way from home."

The children looked over the side of the ship. Wildbeard was right. They were surrounded by ocean. There was no sign of land.

Emily sighed. "So, what do we do now?" she asked.

Wildbeard reached inside his beard and pulled out an old yellow scroll. "We hunt for treasure," he said. "That's what!"

CHAPTER 4   The Treasure Map

Wildbeard rolled out his map.

"I'm looking for a treasure chest," the pirate explained. "One that belonged to my mother!"

He pulled out a picture of an elderly lady. She was wearing a pirate hat and had a beard that was even bigger than the Captain's!

"What's inside the chest?" Jacob asked.

"Mind your own business!" Wildbeard snapped. He really was a very grumpy pirate.

Emily looked at the map. It showed a small island with a cross in the middle.

"X marks the spot?" she asked. "Is that where the treasure is buried?"

Wildbeard didn't have a chance to answer. Suddenly, the ship began to shake. Waves crashed against its side and water slopped onto the deck.

"It's a storm," squeaked Frank in panic.

Wildbeard groaned. "No, it's not," he said sadly.

"What do you mean?" Jacob asked. He was hanging onto the mast to steady himself.

"It's my beard," Wildbeard told them.
"It's cursed."

"It's what?" Emily asked, not believing her ears.

Wildbeard nodded. "As long as I have this beard, I'm doomed to be attacked by sea monsters. That's why I needed this ship. Mine was shipwrecked."

"Then why don't you just shave off your beard?" Frank asked.

Wildbeard glared at the hamster. "A pirate without a beard? Don't be ridiculous!"

The ship nearly tipped over into the sea. Everyone slid across the wet deck and crashed into the side.

Before they could get up, giant tentacles burst out of the water.

They wrapped around the ship and started to squeeze.

"It's a sea monster!" squeaked Frank. "And it's going to crush us!"

Emily peered over the side of the ship.

The monster was below them. It had horrible red eyes and a sharp beak for a mouth.

"No monster is going to keep Captain Wildbeard from his treasure," the pirate shouted.

He rushed towards one of the tentacles and jabbed it with his cutlass.

The sword just wobbled and bent.

"Your cutlass is made of rubber?" Jacob gasped.

"Mummy always said I wasn't old enough to have a real one," Wildbeard said as a slimy tentacle wrapped around him.

"Help!" he cried. "It's got me!"

"It's got us all!" shouted Frank.

The sea monster shook the ship, throwing the children from their feet.

Frank screamed in terror as he tumbled over the side of the boat.

"Frank!" Emily called after him. She looked at Jacob in panic. "He can't swim!"

Jacob grabbed a rope and tossed it into the water.

"Frank, grab this!" he shouted down to the hamster.

Frank caught hold of the rope and climbed back up.

"That was horrible," he spluttered, shivering on the deck. "Look at me. I'm like a drowned rat… or… hamster!"

"We're all going to end up in the water if we don't do something quickly," Jacob said.

Emily had an idea. "Chips," she said excitedly.

"This is no time to think of food!" Wildbeard yelled, still trapped in the tentacle's grip.

"No, you don't understand," Emily said. She turned to her soggy hamster.

"Frank, you had a saltcellar in your cheeks earlier. Do you have a pepper pot too?"

"Of course," Frank said. He reached into his cheek and pulled out a small container. "Here it is."

Emily took the pot and started pouring pepper over the side of the ship. It sprinkled into the sea monster's massive face.

The sea monster sniffed.

Its eyes watered.

Its head shook.

It opened its beak and...

"AAAA–CHOOOOOOO!"

The sea monster sneezed. It was the biggest sneeze you've ever heard.

It blew the pirate ship out of the monster's tentacles and up into the air. Even Wildbeard was blown free.

"Here we go again," wailed Frank as the ship soared through the sky.

"But where are we going to land this time?" asked Jacob.

CHAPTER 6   X Marks the Spot

The ship started to drop.

"Land ahoy!" shouted Wildbeard. "There's a desert island beneath us!"

Emily just had time to look up before the ship crashed into a golden beach.

THUMP!

The ship broke into a thousand pieces, but Wildbeard didn't care. He was jumping up and down on his peg legs.

"Look!" he said, excitedly.

Wildbeard pulled three shovels out of his beard. There was a large black cross in the sand.

"What else do you keep in there?" Jacob asked.

"Just start digging," ordered Wildbeard.

Emily's shovel hit something hard. "It's the treasure chest!" she said.

Wildbeard pulled the heavy box out of the sand.

"So, what's inside?" asked Jacob. "Gold? Gems?"

"No," Wildbeard grinned. "Something much better that that!"

He opened the lid and pulled out a small plastic comb.

"Is that it?" Frank said, amazed. "We went through all that for a plastic comb?"

"It belonged to my mum," said Wildbeard, running it through his beard happily. "Nothing untangles hair like Mum's best comb!"

"So that's why you were so grumpy," Emily laughed.

"I hate having a scruffy beard," said Wildbeard.

"But how are we going to get home?" asked Jacob.

"In that!" said Frank, pointing into the sky.

They all looked up. Another pirate ship was flying towards them. It was attached to thousands of floating balloons.

"Ahoy, down there!" called Albert Sparkle-Trousers from the front of the boat. "I'm here to rescue you!"

He threw down a rope. "Climb up!"

"I don't think I want to go onto another pirate ship," Frank sighed.

But Emily was already climbing the rope. "Don't be silly," she said. "Last one on board buys the chips!"

Questions

1. **What was Albert Sparkle-Trousers wearing on his feet?** (*page 8*)

2. **What was Captain Wildbeard wearing when Emily first spotted him?** (*page 13*)

3. **Who did the treasure chest belong to?** (*page 18*)

4. **What is Captain Wildbeard's cutlass made of?** (*page 23*)

5. **How did Emily defeat the sea monster?** (*page 26*)

6. **What did they find in the treasure chest?** (*page 28*)

Meet the Author

Cavan Scott spends his days making up stuff – and he loves it! He's written for *Star Wars*, *Doctor Who*, *Adventure Time*, *Skylanders*, *Angry Birds*, *Penguins of Madagascar* and *The Beano*! He lives in Bristol with his wife, daughters and an inflatable Dalek called Desmond!

Meet the Illustrator

Abby Ryder is a cartoonist who loves comic books and video games. Her greatest life ambition is to one day become best friends with a giant robot.